D1523799

HARBORED IN HAWAII

RAMBLING RV COZY MYSTERIES, BOOK 13

PATTI BENNING

SUMMER PRESCOTT BOOKS PUBLISHING

CHAPTER ONE

Spring in Michigan was chilly and damp and felt like a miracle after the long winter. Tulia Blake could hardly wait to get away from it.

"I'm only going to be gone for ten days," she told her best friend, the beloved creature who had grown up alongside her and had been there for every single one of her ups and downs.

Her African Grey parrot, Cicero, preened a strand of her hair with his beak as she stroked the soft feathers on his back.

"I know," she murmured. "It sounds like a long time, but it will fly by in a flash, you'll see. I'm sorry I can't take you with me, but it's not easy to bring animals into Hawaii, even just for a visit. You'll be staying here with Mom and Dad, and I promise I'll video call you."

She had finished her trip around the United States almost six months ago and had spent that time split between staying with her parents and visiting Loon Bay, Massachusetts, where her long-distance boyfriend lived and worked as a private investigator, along with his business partner, Marc. In between going back and forth between Michigan and Massachusetts and catching up with her friends and family, Tulia had started work on creating a charity and further preparing for her future as a millionaire. It had been almost a year since she won the lottery, and sometimes it still didn't feel real.

Her life had changed when she got the money, but the real changes came during her long trip around the country. She had seen and experienced things she hadn't even dreamed of during her sheltered life as a homebody. Not all of it had been good, but both good and bad, her experiences had made her realize how much *more* there was to the world.

It was nice to be back home again, and she *had* missed her parents and her friends, but she had been growing increasingly hungry for new experiences again.

Which was why the Hawaii trip had been

conceived of. She wasn't ready to commit to more months on the road quite yet, but she wanted to go somewhere new, somewhere *different.* She was still waiting on her passport to come in, but the United States of America had a lot to offer within its borders, and Hawaii fit the bill for 'different.'

She wasn't going alone, either. Samuel, Marc, and Marc's wife, Violet, would all be meeting her there. Samuel and Marc deserved a vacation; they had been working hard to get their business up and running, and some time off would do them good. The winter had been busy for all of them, just not busy in the ways Tulia preferred.

One day, she would finish visiting all fifty states. Today—or tomorrow, technically; it was a *long* flight —she would knock Hawaii off that list.

"Be good," she told her bird, pressing a quick kiss to the top of his feathery head. "I'll be back before you know it."

She swallowed against a lump in her throat as she put Cicero back in his cage. It was a new cage, the largest she could fit inside her parents' living room. Staying with them whenever she wasn't visiting Loon Bay had been … interesting. Not *bad,* but she was selfishly looking forward to having her own place again. Still, she appreciated them giving her a place to stay while she got her life in order. She just wished they would let her help more financially. She wanted to pay off their house and help them retire in luxury, but they insisted that her winnings were *hers*. Even paying for the occasional meal out was a battle she didn't always win.

Leaving Cicero behind felt bad, but she didn't want the bird to see how upset she was, so she turned away and grabbed her suitcase. Her carry-on—a ridiculously large purse that held all of her essentials and then some—was already waiting for her by the door. Or, it *was*. It was gone when she entered the entrance hallway, and her father stepped back through the front door and gestured for her to hand him the handle of her suitcase.

"I'm getting the car loaded up," he said. "Your mother is in the kitchen, packing some snacks."

"She knows I can't bring anything she makes me on the plane, right?"

Her father chuckled. "The snacks are for us, not you. We've got two hours in the car, and you know how your mother is about stopping for fast food when we don't need to."

She handed her suitcase over so he could take it out to the car, then pulled the closet open to take her most comfortable pair of sneakers out. The airport was an hour away, and that was just the beginning of her journey. She wasn't looking forward to spending hours on a plane and was already wishing she had splurged on a first-class ticket, but she was trying to be responsible with her money and not end up broke and destitute like so many other lottery winners did. Her financial adviser had drilled in just how quickly even millions could vanish if she spent to her heart's content. Her fancy RV had been her one big purchase, and it was one she didn't regret, but she tried to live a mostly normal life other than that.

A few minutes later, all three of them were bundled into the car. Tulia sat in the back, with a cooler full of snacks on one side of her and her carry-on on the other side. With her parents chatting up front and her father's favorite radio station playing quietly in the background, the entire experience brought her back to the rare trips they took when she was a child. *It's crazy how much my life has changed*, she thought. *And how much it has stayed the same.*

She hugged both of her parents goodbye when they pulled up to the departures entrance to the Detroit Metro Airport. Telling them goodbye wasn't as difficult as saying goodbye to Cicero had been, because her parents, at least, understood where she was going and that she would be back before too long. She left her mom with instructions to spoil the bird and promised both of them she would take plenty of pictures. Then, with her carry-on over one shoulder and the handle of her suitcase clasped in her other hand, she dragged her luggage into the airport and started the long process of checking her bags, going through security, and finding her gate.

The flight was nearly ten hours long, so she spent as much time on her feet as she could before boarding. She had paid a little extra to reserve a window seat, and had packed a comfortable neck pillow, a book, and her laptop into her carry-on, all of which she tucked under the seat in front of her as she waited for takeoff.

As the plane's wheels left the asphalt, she peered out the window, looking down as the ground dropped away. Leaving like this didn't give her quite the same sense of adventure that setting out in her RV had, but it was close. She would still technically be in the United States, but she would be an ocean away from the rest of the country, farther than she had ever been.

She had ten days of vacation to look forward to. Ten days to relax in a small resort on a beach in Hawaii with her friends.

This was going to be an awesome trip.

CHAPTER TWO

Even though she managed to sleep for half the flight, Tulia felt exhausted when the plane landed in Maui. She grabbed her carry-on and shuffled down the aisle, following the rest of the passengers as they disembarked from the plane into the Kahului Airport. The time change didn't help. Hawaii was six hours behind Michigan time, which meant that while her internal clock told her it should be the middle of the night, locally, it was just midevening.

She texted Samuel as she made her way to the baggage claim and waited for her suitcase to appear. She snatched it off the carousel, double-checked that it was, in fact, hers, then rolled it behind her to the arrivals exit.

Three familiar faces were waiting for her by the doors.

"Hey, Tulia," Marc said, waving at her.

His wife, Violet, beamed. "I'm glad your flight wasn't delayed, a few others were, so we were getting worried. It's a shame we couldn't all fly together."

Samuel gave her a tight hug before pulling back and saying, "We landed about forty-five minutes ago. How was your flight?"

"Boring, which is probably a good thing to say about a flight, but I'm still glad it's over." She went up on her tiptoes to kiss him. It was always good to see him again. Maintaining a long-distance relationship was hard work, but the connection she and Samuel had made it worth it. "How was your trip?"

"Cramped, but worth it," Samuel said. He took her suitcase for her. "I'm glad you added my name to the rental car listing. We went and picked it up while we waited for you."

"Oh, good." She wrinkled her nose. "I'd be lying if I said I was looking forward to sitting down again, but at least the car should have more legroom than the airplane did."

The four of them left the airport and found the rental car where Samuel had parked it in the short-term parking lot. It was a small SUV with just enough room in the back to stuff Tulia's suitcase in on top of everyone else's luggage. She was glad when Marc insisted she take the passenger seat in front, since he wanted to sit with Violet in the back. The legroom was much appreciated, as was the view out the windshield.

"Wow," she breathed, looking at the tropical trees that had been planted around the airport. "It reminds me of being in Florida, a little, but it feels different."

"My sister went to Hawaii for her honeymoon," Violet said from the back as Samuel pulled out of the parking lot. Tulia typed the address of the resort into her phone as she listened to the other woman. "She went to a different island than we're staying on, but she loved her trip. She made me promise to bring her back some souvenirs."

"I'm glad the three of you convinced me to come along," Marc said. "I was reluctant to take a hiatus from work, but I think this is going to be worth it."

"I've got to admit, it feels good to be traveling again," Samuel commented, glancing at her phone screen when she held it up so he could see the map. "Last year had its ups and downs, but it was probably the best year of my life."

"Other than the kidnapping and near-death experiences," Tulia muttered.

He grimaced. "Yeah, I could have gone without those. But we did a lot of good in the world."

Tulia couldn't argue with that. She sat back in the seat and enjoyed the scenery going by as they drove through the gorgeous Hawaiian landscape. The little she saw from the car looked like paradise. She had done a lot of research on the islands of Hawaii before booking the trip, and she was excited to see more of it up close and personal.

She had looked over a few options for resorts, and had finally settled on a small, luxurious resort on its own private slice of beach east of Kahului. It wasn't cheap, but her friends had refused to let her pay for it on her own, and they had ended up splitting the cost four ways—though, she was determined to treat them to a few surprises while they were here. The resort was about forty minutes away from the airport, and the sun was beginning to go down as they pulled into the driveway, painting the sky in oranges, pinks, and purples.

Flowers and trees lined the drive, and the resort itself was a large, white building with a beautiful red terra-cotta roof. It was shaped like a horseshoe with a pool in the center of the courtyard that looked out to the beach and the ocean. When they stepped through the front doors, the interior was just as light and airy as the exterior was, and there were flowers everywhere, so many that the air itself smelled sweet.

Tulia had the confirmation email ready, so their check-in went smoothly, and a bellhop was waiting to help them with their luggage. She had reserved two suites for them on the top floor, so they would be right across the hall from each other. Violet looked thrilled as they rode the elevator up, and seeing the happiness on her friend's face made Tulia smile. She had become close to the other woman in the past few months, and it always made her happy to see her friends happy.

When she and Samuel entered their suite, the view took her breath away. The wall was decorated in colors that matched the sunset: oranges and pale purples and yellows. It was absolutely beautiful, and Tulia set her bags down before stepping out onto the balcony to take it all in.

"I love Michigan, but this place is a million times more beautiful than Midland ever could be," she murmured.

"Yeah," Samuel said quietly from beside her. "Loon Bay has its charm, and I love the New England area, but this island feels too beautiful to be real."

They explored the rest of the suite—Tulia could hardly wait to take a bath in the large corner tub—and unpacked their bags before venturing across the hall to see how Marc and Violet were doing.

When Tulia stepped out in the hall, a middle-aged woman was walking past them from the direction of the stairs. She gave Tulia a quick smile, then spotted Samuel, and her smile brightened.

"Oh, how lovely," the woman said. "Please tell me if I'm being too nosy, but are the two of you here on a honeymoon?"

Tulia shook her head. "Just a vacation," she said. "Do you work here?"

The woman laughed. "No, no, not at all. I'm here on a working vacation. I'm a writer, you see, and I'm planning my next book. A murder mystery. I've been suffering from writer's block and had a bunch of points saved up with the airline I use, so I decided to get away for a week and see if I could make inspiration strike. I'm always curious about other people and what their stories are. I take inspiration from everything I see and do." She extended her hand. "I'm Carrie Tucker."

Tulia shook her hand. "I'm Tulia Blake. Are you here on your own?"

"Yep," she said cheerfully. "I like traveling alone. I get to spend my vacations doing what I want, when I want, and while I love my husband, he's quite the homebody and tends to spend most of any trip we go on worrying about what's going on back home."

"I get it," Tulia said. "I took a road trip around the United States mostly on my own. I was gone for months. It was hard and a little frightening at first, but it was also one of the most amazing and inspiring things I've ever done."

Carrie's eyes brightened. "I'd love to talk to you some more and hear about some of the places you've been to. I don't want to interfere with your trip, though."

"I wouldn't mind meeting up for a chat," Tulia said. This was one of the things she loved about traveling—meeting new people and making new friends. "How much longer will you be here for?"

"I just flew in yesterday, so for another six days. I signed up for snorkeling tomorrow morning, and I think there are still spots left, if you want to join me. Beginners are welcome."

"I'll talk to the rest of my group and see if they're interested," Tulia said. "I write a blog, and I'd really love the chance to talk to you too, to compare notes, and maybe get your email address."

"I'm staying just a few rooms down from you. Even if you don't go snorkeling tomorrow, come find me. It sounds like we have a lot in common. I don't meet a lot of other female writers who also travel on their own. I'll let you get going now, but it was nice to meet you, Tulia."

She waved and continued on down the hallway. Tulia watched her go, then turned back to Samuel, who looked amused. He had been completely sidelined during the conversation, and Tulia only realized it now.

"Sorry," she said, feeling her cheeks heating up.

Samuel chuckled. "Snorkeling sounds good to me."

She smiled. "Let's see what Marc and Violet think. We *are* here with them, and I don't want to make decisions without talking to them first."

"I can guarantee you that Violet will be interested in snorkeling. And Marc will probably be happy to do whatever the rest of us are doing. Besides, we have over a week here. There will be plenty of time to do everything each of us wants to."

She grinned as she knocked on Marc and Violet's door. It felt great to be back in the swing of things. This trip was shaping up to be one of her best yet.

CHAPTER THREE

Everyone was excited about the idea of going
snorkeling in the morning. In retrospect, she shouldn't
have been surprised—they were in Hawaii, on a
beach. What better way to get their feet wet than to
see the ocean in all of its glory?

They got dinner at the restaurant attached to the
resort, where Tulia and Violet shared two entrées that
they both desperately wanted to try. Samuel got one
of the fanciest burgers Tulia had ever seen—it had a
pineapple on it, and she had to try a bite out of morbid
curiosity—while Marc treated himself to a steak. By
the time they returned to their rooms, Tulia was
utterly exhausted. Her internal clock told her it was
the early hours of the morning, and it had been a very,
very long day. She hoped that by going to bed at a

reasonable time according to the local clock, and sleeping through the night, her jet leg wouldn't be too bad the next day. She wanted to enjoy every moment of this trip.

She changed into her pajamas and left the bedroom window open to let the warm, pleasant breeze in, then collapsed on the mattress. It felt like a cloud, and her last thought before falling asleep was to wonder what brand of mattresses the resort used.

It wasn't like she could *never* treat herself to something expensive, and a mattress this comfortable would be worth the price.

She only felt a little out of it when she woke up the next morning. Snorkeling wasn't until ten, so there was no hurry to get ready. She took her time in the shower, then put on her bathing suit under a pair of shorts and a loose blouse before tying her hair up into a ponytail. It felt strange not to have Cicero waiting for his breakfast. She hated not being able to bring him along, but even if Hawaii made it easy to bring pets on vacation, she knew the long flight wouldn't have been comfortable for him. She would see him again soon, and she knew he would be well cared for at home.

She and Samuel waited for Marc and Violet to join them in the hallway, then made their way downstairs to get breakfast at the resort's restaurant. The fresh fruit platter was the best Tulia had ever tasted, and the bacon and pineapple bake she ordered out of curiosity was pretty good too. She could hardly wait to taste more of Hawaii's local cuisine. There was no shortage of restaurants on the island, and while the resort's food hadn't disappointed so far, she wasn't about to limit herself to only eating here.

"So, how are your plans for the move coming along?" Marc asked her across the table as they ate. Tulia sipped her drink—a cold, floral tea that she had been promised had caffeine in it—while she mentally reviewed where she was in the process.

"The apartment I'm going to move into won't be available until the end of June," she said. "I finalized the lease on it a few days ago, so that's done, at least. I'm going to need to transfer banks, since the bank I use doesn't have a branch in Massachusetts. That's going to be a pain, though my financial advisor is helping me with that. I'm still looking into what it will take to get a new driver's license and all the other fiddly details involved in moving to a different state. It's more complicated than I expected."

"So, if your apartment is available at the end of June, does that mean you'll be moving in about two months?" Violet asked. "That's so soon. It will be nice to have you in the area all the time. Are you nervous? It's a big change."

"Not really," Tulia admitted. "I've visited enough that I'm familiar with the town by now, and after traveling so much last year, I already know I'll be able to adjust from being away from Michigan. Honestly, I'm looking forward to it. It'll be nice to see everyone more often."

She shot a grin at Samuel, the man who had followed her across the country and saved her life as many times as she had saved his. Their history together was far from simple, but it had forged a connection between them she had never felt with anyone else.

He smiled back at her, his eyes no less pleased than her own expression was. "I still feel a little bad you're the one moving, but I won't lie—I'm looking forward to it just as much as you are."

"You already agreed it makes the most sense," she pointed out. "You and Marc run a business together. You can't move away from that. And I've been wanting to move out of Michigan almost since I first set out on my road trip. I like Massachusetts, and I love Loon Bay. It's the perfect location, as far as I'm concerned. Right next to the ocean, close to Boston, and with tons of that New England charm.

Honestly, the only thing I'm not looking forward to is the move itself. Deciding what to bring, what to sell, and what to put into storage is hard, and I know I'm going to regret some of my choices when I finally get there."

They continued chatting about Loon Bay through breakfast and as they walked down to the beach afterward. There was a small hut for the snorkeling and surfing equipment with a cute thatch roof, and a few people were already gathered around it. Carrie was one of them, and she waved brightly before coming over to them.

"Tulia! I'm glad you made it."

"Thanks for suggesting snorkeling," she said. "We're all looking forward to it. Has inspiration struck yet?"

The other woman shook her head with a small smile. "Not yet, but I'm still enjoying myself, so I'm not too beat up over it."

Tulia introduced her to the others, and the five of them made small talk while they waited. There were two other women standing near the hut, both with long auburn hair and similar enough features that Tulia suspected they were related. The younger of the two women had a male companion who occasionally looked in her direction but hung back other than that, more focused on his cell phone than on what was going on around him.

A few minutes before ten, a man wearing swim trunks and carrying a clipboard came down from the resort.

"Is this everyone for snorkeling?" he called out. Conversation died down as they turned toward him. "I'm going to call your names. Please indicate who you are when you hear yours. Veronica Gibson?"

The older of the two women Tulia hadn't met yet raised her hand. "That's me."

The man made a mark on his clipboard. "Rebecca Gibson?" The younger of the two women indicated herself, and Travis smiled at her a bit longer than he had at her sister before he moved on. "Jay Armitage?" The man next to Rebecca waved with a smile. "Carrie Tucker?"

"Present," she said cheerfully.

"Tulia Blake?" He continued down the list through Violet's name, then said, "I'm Travis Feeney, and I'm going to be your guide today. I've been snorkeling and scuba diving for over a decade. There are a few basic rules we have to go through before I start passing out equipment. Before we get to that, I need everyone to sign a waiver. I'll pass the clipboard around – each of you will need to initial twice and sign once on the sheet. Please print your name on the top of it."

Tulia scanned over the waiver when it reached her. It seemed basic enough, about the resort not being responsible for any injuries or accidents they received during the activity. She signed her name before passing it on.

Once they were finished, Travis said, "Now, who here has snorkeling experience? I'll get you into the water first, then I'll work with the beginners separately. I'd like to remind all of you not to touch anything. This is a protected environment, and some sea life can be dangerous. Don't take anything other than memories—or photographs, if you have an underwater camera. Please do not swim past the drop off, and be cautious around the rocks that are sticking up out of the surf over there. They are slippery and dangerous, and I ask that no one tries to climb on them or swim through them. Don't get too far from the rest of the group on your own, and don't swim out past the reef."

Tulia had gone snorkeling in Florida, so she and Carrie were the only ones with enough experience for Travis to hand them their swim fins, snorkels, and goggles and send them off into the water. Tulia kept close to Carrie as they made their way down the beach toward the waves.

"Do you snorkel a lot?" she asked the other woman.

"I've been a few times," Carrie said. "I try to travel somewhere new every year. It's one of the reasons I love my job—I can work from anywhere. This is my first time in Hawaii, though. Isn't this water just gorgeous?"

It really was. The water was crystal clear and felt like it belonged in a movie rather than in real life. It was refreshingly cool on Tulia's skin, and she waded in until it was deep enough that she could swim. She ducked her face under as soon as she could. Underwater was even more gorgeous than above it. The white sand extended away from the shore, until it was replaced with fields of kelp and seaweed, other underwater plants Tulia couldn't identify, and beyond that, there was a rocky reef where schools of fish swam and darted around the outcroppings.

She and Carrie swam near each other, occasionally popping up above the water to chat or point out something beneath the waves. After a while, they both paddled in place and glanced back at the beach.

"I thought they'd be out here by now," Tulia

mused. She could see the group still gathered around the hut. "I wonder if something happened."

"I can go back and see," Carrie volunteered. "I need to reapply my sunscreen anyway." She grimaced. "There's a history of skin cancer in my family. I don't mess around with sunburns."

Tulia hesitated. They weren't supposed to go off on their own. Before she could respond, the group by the hut started moving toward the water. She would be fine for the minute or two it took them to reach her, so she waved Carrie off and ducked her head back underwater.

They had nine days left of their trip. Tulia was already hoping that they would have time to go snorkeling at least once more, because as gorgeous as the beaches of Hawaii were, beneath the waves was an entirely different world, and one she couldn't get enough of.

CHAPTER FOUR

"What took so long?" Tulia asked from where she was treading water just past standing depth.

Samuel grimaced as he swam over to her, looking unusually annoyed. "One of the other guests, the one named Jay, took a call in the middle of Travis's instructions. Travis had to wait until he ended the call to continue."

"It was rude," Violet muttered as she splashed over to them. "But we're out here now, so I guess it doesn't matter. Let's go see some fish!"

Though they all swam in the same area, Tulia's group and Rebecca, Jay, and Veronica's stayed separate. Carrie spent most of her time near Tulia's group, but swam over to the other one occasionally, and Travis split his attention between all of them at first, but after a few minutes, he seemed to focus completely on Rebecca. Every time Tulia looked around, he was with the younger of the two sisters, and they seemed to be moving further and further away from the group. Tulia had a blast despite the lack of help from their guide, and from the way her friends were grinning, she could tell they were enjoying themselves too.

As time went on, some of the others began to go back to the beach. Rebecca was the first to swim away, and before too long, Veronica mentioned that she was getting tired. Jay left shortly after they did, and Carrie grumbled about having to reapply her sunscreen again before kicking back toward the shore. Travis stayed out with Tulia's group for another twenty minutes before saying, "All right, unfortunately, that's as much time as we have today. Feel free to sign up for snorkeling again tomorrow, though. We also offer scuba diving certification classes, if anyone is interested."

As they swam back toward the beach, Tulia realized how hungry she was. Swimming took a lot of energy, and she had been out for over an hour. She took her swim fins off once her feet touched the sand and walked back up the beach with Samuel. Marc and Violet trailed behind, looking at pictures on the waterproof camera Violet had thought ahead enough to purchase from the resort's front desk.

"I say we go into town for lunch," Tulia suggested to Samuel. "We can find a nice restaurant to eat at. I'm in the mood for sushi, myself."

"I wouldn't mind a bowl of ramen," Samuel said. "I'm sure there's a good Japanese restaurant in the area." He turned around to ask Marc and Violet what they thought, and they both agreed that Japanese food sounded good. They started walking back toward the hut to return their gear, only stopping when Travis hurried down the beach toward them, his face pale.

"Have either of you seen Rebecca?" he asked. "I thought she returned to the beach early, but both her sister and her fiancé say they haven't seen her."

Tulia looked toward the hut, where Carrie, Veronica, and Jay were all waiting.

But no Rebecca.

"I haven't seen her," Tulia said.

"She might have gone back to the resort," Samuel said. "She was the first one to swim back. Did you see her supplies in the hut?"

"I checked when I realized she was missing," Travis said. "I thought she might've returned to the resort too, but her gear is still gone."

Tulia and Samuel exchanged a worried look.

"Maybe she went further along the beach," Marc suggested. "We should split up and look for her."

"Samuel and I can go back into the water," Tulia suggested, already putting her swim fins back on.

"That should be my job," Travis objected.

"I have snorkeling experience already, and Samuel's a strong swimmer," Tulia pointed out. "The more people who are looking, the better. If she went back into the water, she could be in trouble."

Travis hesitated, then nodded. "Right. I need to phone up to the resort to make sure she isn't there. Maybe she brought her gear with her, for some reason. I'll catch up to you soon."

"Violet and I will walk along the beach and look for her," Marc said. "Be careful, you two."

Tulia nodded. She and Samuel hurried back into the water, and Tulia ducked down beneath the waves as soon as she could. Samuel stayed above the water, calling out for Rebecca.

"I don't see her anywhere," Tulia said when she came back up. The others had spread out along the beach, and they all seemed to still be looking for her. Tulia turned around in the water, trying to figure out where the missing woman would have gone. Her eyes landed on the rocks that were poking out over the waves by the reef. "We should go that way. If she was swimming and got a cramp, maybe she went to the rocks so she would have something to hang onto while she took a break."

"Good idea," Samuel said.

They swam over together, Tulia ducking her head beneath the waves every once in a while to look underwater. She still couldn't get over how clear it was, but it didn't make finding Rebecca any easier. The rocky reef rose close to the surface of the water, which made it hard to swim as they approached it. Tulia's swim fins kept scraping across the rocks, and she scared a school of curious fish away with her splashing. She was getting more and more worried about Rebecca as time went on and no one had seen her. She and Samuel both kept glancing toward the beach, hoping to see the others waving them back, but no one had found her yet.

Carefully, Tulia climbed onto one of the rocks. It was slippery and jagged, and Samuel braced himself on the rocks beneath the waves to steady her.

"Do you see anything?" he asked.

"Not yet. Rebecca?" she called out, moving higher so she could look into the spaces between the rocks. "Are you—" She broke off when she saw a pale form floating in the water between two of the larger rocks.

"I see her, Samuel," she said. She reached down to take off her swim fins so she could climb down the other side of the rock more easily. She slid into the water next to Rebecca, wincing as one of the sharp edges of another rock scratched her shin. The pain was easy to ignore when she realized how still the other woman was, and that she was floating face down in the water.

Carefully, she turned the other woman over. Her eyes were open, but she was unresponsive.

"Samuel," she called out. "Help me."

Between the two of them they managed to drag her on top of the rock. Tulia had taken a course on first aid back when she worked as a waitress, but all of her knowledge seemed to flood out of her as she stared at the woman lying on the rock in front of her. Samuel was the one who started CPR on her, and while he tried to get her breathing again Tulia stood up, waving frantically with both arms at the people on the beach.

It took a long moment for one of them to see her. She saw the person—Violet, she recognized the other woman's bathing suit—wave at her, then turn and gesture at someone else before pointing toward her. The second person hurried into the hut and rushed out a moment later with a life vest on and emergency flotation device in his hand. He dove into the water and Tulia knelt beside Samuel and Rebecca. She still wasn't moving, and Tulia had a horrible, sinking feeling that no matter how long Samuel continued CPR, she wasn't ever going to move again.

Carefully, she brushed some of the woman's wet hair out of her eyes, then froze. There was a bloodied wound on her temple. Tulia was no private investigator or police detective, but even she could tell that the injury was a serious one.

It might not have killed her on its own, but it might explain why Rebecca had drowned.

CHAPTER FIVE

The group that returned to Tulia's suite was much more somber than they had been when they went down to the beach. After Rebecca's body was recovered and emergency services called, they all waited on the sand for the police and paramedics to arrive. Travis had taken over CPR, but everyone already knew it was too late.

Rebecca's sister, Veronica, had to be restrained by Marc as she tried to reach her sister's body, and Jay, Rebecca's fiancé, had simply stared in silence that was almost as bad as Veronica's tears.

Even Carrie had looked disturbed as she watched, and Tulia wondered what it was like for someone who wrote about death so much to actually witness the aftermath of one.

Samuel held the door as Marc and Violet entered, then shut it behind them, turning the deadbolt for good measure. The four of them took a moment to get settled in the suite's living area. Tulia pulled the desk chair out, while Marc and Violet took the couch. Samuel kept to his feet, pacing slowly back and forth across the floor.

"That poor woman," Violet said with a shudder after they had all been silent for a little too long. "I can't even imagine… She went on the vacation of a lifetime, and it ended up being the last thing she ever did."

"What I'm wondering is what she was doing over there by those rocks," Marc said, exchanging a look with Samuel. The two of them had been partners for a long time, and sometimes Tulia was a little jealous of how well they could read each other.

"I was wondering the same thing," Samuel said. "The instructor—Travis—explicitly told us not to go over there, and she wasn't an experienced snorkeler, so I doubt she would have been confident enough to be reckless."

"When was the last time anyone remembers seeing her?" Tulia asked. "I know she was the first one to go back, but did anyone actually see her get to the beach? And why did she get out of the water so early? Was she feeling ill or upset about something?"

"She and her sister got into an argument when Jay took the call that delayed Travis's instructions," Violet chimed in. "I wasn't trying to eavesdrop, but they weren't exactly being quiet. Jay is Rebecca's fiancé, and Veronica blamed her for how rude Jay was being. The rocks might have seemed like a good place for her to sit and collect herself if she was still upset from the call and the argument."

"I can't say I'm impressed with the instructor," Marc said. "It was his job to make sure everyone was safe. He shouldn't have let anyone go off on their own, and he should've noticed as soon as someone went missing. Even if this was an accident, he is still at fault."

"What do you mean *if* this was an accident?" Violet asked, turning toward her husband.

"Did you see how her fiancé reacted?" Marc asked. "He barely seemed to respond to the sight of her lying on the sand. That's not what I would expect from someone seeing the body of a loved one." He glanced at Samuel, who nodded. Tulia found herself nodding too.

"He barely reacted. But that could have been shock." She frowned. "Just because he didn't react how you might expect doesn't mean he had anything to do with her death. Samuel and I both climbed up those rocks to get to her body, and they were extremely slippery. I can see how she might have climbed onto them, only to slip and hit her head on the way down."

"As much as I hate to say it, speculating isn't going to help anything," Samuel said. He looked a little reluctant as he spoke but soldiered on. "We aren't here for work. We're taking a vacation, and we don't have any evidence that her accident was anything but what it appears. We've already given our statements to the police, and that's as far as our involvement should go. The local authorities won't appreciate some nosy tourists getting involved."

"I'm with Samuel on this one, sweetie," Violet said, patting Marc's knee. "You promised me you wouldn't work while we were here. The police are already doing their own investigation, and I'm sure the resort will investigate as well."

"All right," Marc said with a sigh. "I know I promised to leave my job at home. We'll let the local authorities do their jobs, and I'll try to focus on enjoying the rest of the trip."

It didn't sit quite right with Tulia, but what was the alternative? They were in another state, one with its own laws and customs. Hawaii was the most foreign place she had been, for all that it was still a part of the United States. And there might not even be anything for them *to* investigate. Rebecca's death might truly have been an unfortunate accident.

"I agree, we should try to focus on the trip," she said at last. "I'm not sure what the resort is going to do about what happened. It sounds like the beach is closed down indefinitely, and the staff will probably be distracted. We should try to keep out of their hair as much as possible and find things to do away from the resort."

"I really want to go on a nature hike," Violet said. "It's so beautiful here. I think we should look through the pamphlets and each make a list of the things we want to do. Then we can compare notes and make a schedule. But first … we should eat. I can't believe I have an appetite after what happened, but I'm starving."

Tulia was hungry too, and the guys made sounds of agreement. It seemed that even a tragedy couldn't dampen the appetite all the calories they had burned swimming gave them.

"Let's call room service," she suggested. "We can all eat together and start looking through the pamphlets." She forced a smile. "We've still got over a week left here. Let's try our best to have some fun."

After they put in their room service orders, Tulia volunteered to go get some ice from the ice machine down the hall so they could chill the bottle of wine they had ordered along with their meal. She grabbed the ice bucket, then left the room, closing the door to the sound of chatter as the others started looking through the pamphlets. She was glad everyone was still determined to enjoy the trip, but the memory of Rebecca's body floating in the water weighed on her.

She knew she would have nightmares tonight. There was nothing she could do about it, though. She stepped into the hall and looked around, then headed toward where the elevator was, figuring the ice machine was probably somewhere near there. As she walked past the staircase, the door opened, and Carrie came into the hall, her face a little flushed from the exertion of climbing the stairs.

"Oh, Tulia," she said, coming to a halt. "Are you leaving early, or are you going to keep staying here? I just saw quite a few guests checking out downstairs, which is why I'm asking."

Tulia paused, cradling the ice bucket in her arms. "We're staying. How about you?"

"I'm staying too," Carrie said. "This is going to

make me sound like a monster, but I have so many ideas for my new book. I'm just about to go write them down. What happened is horrible, of course, but I've never felt so inspired."

"That probably isn't something you should admit," Tulia replied. "But we just decided to continue on with our vacation and try to enjoy it despite what happened, so I can't judge you too harshly."

Carrie smiled at her. "I knew I liked you. There's something to be said for pragmatism. Anyway, some of the other guests and myself are meeting at a restaurant in town tomorrow for lunch. Do you and your friends want to join us? I just came back from the lobby, and the resort is shutting down all scheduled activities for the foreseeable future, so there isn't much else to do here besides sleep and eat."

"I'll talk to the others," Tulia said. "What restaurant and when?"

"Leilani's Bistro at noon. Come if you can, but if not, I'll see you around."

Tulia nodded and watched as Carrie continued on to her room. She eyed the stairs for a moment, wondering why the woman had taken them instead of the elevator, then continued on in her quest for ice.

She was a little unsettled at how casually Carrie

seemed to be taking Rebecca's death, but she couldn't judge the other woman, not when she was about to eat a delicious meal and plan out the rest of her trip with her friends. Everyone had their own ways of coping with tragedies.

CHAPTER SIX

It felt good to get out of the cloying atmosphere of the resort. Everything had changed since Rebecca's death the day before. Tulia understood why, and it would have been worse if everyone was ignoring what happened and continuing on with their vacations like nothing was wrong, but it didn't mean that the air in the resort didn't feel suffocating every time she left her suite.

The restaurant Carrie had told her about was a little bistro near the town center. The majority of its seating was on a patio, which was full of bright flowers and faerie lights, which she thought must make the place look like a wonderland after dark.

It was the middle of the day now, but the bistro still looked inviting. Judging by the delicious smells coming from the little restaurant, they were in for an amazing meal.

"So, Carrie just invited a bunch of other guests at the resort out to eat?" Violet asked as they walked down the sidewalk toward the bistro.

"That's what it sounded like." She lowered her voice. "I'm not sure what to think of her. She's an … interesting person. But it doesn't hurt to be social, and we all agreed we wanted to try a few restaurants instead of just eating at the resort all the time."

Violet lowered her own voice as she responded. "You know why both of the guys were so quick to agree, don't you?"

Tulia's lips twitched. "Of course. Despite everything they said yesterday, they're still hoping to get some answers about what happened, and Carrie might have noticed something we didn't. I can't say I blame them. I'm curious too."

Violet groaned. "You're just as bad as they are. I can't believe I thought you would be the sane one in our little group when I first met you."

"You wouldn't have married Marc if you didn't share his passion for mysteries at least a little."

Violet laughed, but then her expression fell. "I love that he's so passionate about what he does, and I've always enjoyed talking about his work and sharing theories with him, but after he got shot last year, things changed. I always knew his job could be dangerous, but I didn't really *feel it* until he almost died. I know he's not going to retire until he's good and ready, but I do wish he would find something else to be so passionate about. I'm just glad that he works with Samuel. Those two are the best of friends, and I know Samuel will always have his back."

Tulia could understand the other woman's concern. She worried about Samuel too, especially when he was working a homicide or missing persons case. Still, she was no stranger to danger. After all, she had gone on a months-long road trip on her own. She had tried to be smart about it, but there was a certain level of risk inherent in any woman traveling on her own like she had.

While she and Violet got along well and were good friends, where they differed was that Tulia was prepared to accept some risk, while Violet seemed to hate living with any amount of it.

She opened the door to the bistro and gestured the other woman through. Samuel held the door for her as she and Marc went through, then fell into step behind her.

"Was she talking about Marc retiring again?" he asked quietly as they approached the hostess.

"She knows it's not going to happen. She just worries," Tulia said as she looked around the bistro. The hostess approached them, a welcoming smile on her face.

"Hi there! Welcome to Leilani's Bistro. How many will I be seating today?"

"We're actually meeting a group," Tulia said. "I'm not sure if they're already here. Do you mind if we look around for them?"

"I just sat a group out on the patio who said they were waiting for a few more people. Right this way."

They followed her through the bistro to the patio exit, where Tulia spotted Carrie sitting at a large, round table under a sun umbrella. Her steps faltered when she spotted both Veronica and Jay at the table, along with two other people Tulia hadn't met yet. She glanced over at Samuel.

"Okay, I know we said we weren't going to get involved, but going out to a social lunch the day after your sister or fiancé passed away is not normal, is it?"

Samuel's brow furrowed. "No, it is not. Let's keep our eyes and ears peeled."

She saw him look over at Marc and raise his eyebrows, and Marc gave a nod back. Violet looked a little hesitant as they approached the table, sending uncertain looks at Veronica and Jay.

"Tulia!" Carrie exclaimed, waving them over. "I'm glad you made it. We saved seats for you. We already ordered a few appetizers—I figured we could split the bill between all of us?"

"Sounds good to me," Tulia said. She made a mental note to try to swipe the bills from her friends so she could treat them. She appreciated that they weren't just using her for her money, but she wanted to do nice things for them, darn it.

They took their seats. Samuel and Marc were closest to where Veronica and Jay were sitting, with Tulia on Samuel's other side, and Violet between her and the two strangers. Veronica was typing something on her phone, barely even looking up at them, and Jay was just staring down at his drink, slowly turning the glass around and around. Carrie introduced them to the other two people once they were seated.

"This lovely couple are Josiah and Hannah. They were behind me in the check-in line my first day here, and we got to talking." She winked at Tulia. "They are big fans of my books."

"We were so excited to realize we were staying at the same resort as Carrie Tucker," Hannah said. "It's nice to meet you all. What brought you to Hawaii?"

Tulia and her friends introduced themselves and shared a little about their vacation and busy lives. She noticed that Samuel and Marc were careful not to say they were private investigators—they mentioned their business only in vague terms. She exchanged a look with Violet and knew they would both be asking the men about that later. Usually, they were beyond thrilled to talk about their work.

They continued chatting about their experiences so far in Hawaii while they looked over the menus. Both Veronica and Jay remained quiet, and Tulia was itching to know why they were there. She couldn't imagine a world in which she would go out to a casual lunch with strangers the day after losing a loved one.

She might be curious, but she was also hungry. She ordered the grilled mahi mahi sandwich, and quietly promised Violet she would split it with her in exchange for some of her shrimp skewers. It wasn't until after they ordered that Rebecca's death was brought up, and when it was, the topic was broached so bluntly that Tulia nearly inhaled her drink.

"I'm glad you invited us out, Carrie," Hannah said. "I can't believe the resort shut down the beach *and* all of the activities. It's horrible that someone drowned, but this is an expensive place to stay. You'd think they would at least offer us refunds."

Carrie hesitated and glanced over at Veronica and

Jay. Jay was still idly turning his glass around and around on the table, but Veronica's eyes narrowed.

"What did you just say? My *sister* is the one who died. I'm *so* sorry her death was an inconvenience to you."

Hannah's eyes widened, and she exchanged a horrified look with her husband.

"I-I'm sorry. I didn't know you were related to her."

"This is my fault," Carrie cut in. "I should have explained why I invited the eight of you to lunch today."

Tulia frowned. "I didn't know you *had* a reason beyond wanting to get out of the resort."

Carrie leaned forward with her elbows on the table, giving them each a serious look. "As you all know, I am a rather successful author. I write thrillers and mysteries, and as a result, I have a certain way of looking at the world that most people don't. And I'm telling you, I think there was more to Rebecca's death than meets the eye. A lot more."

The table was silent for a moment as they took in her words. Tulia reevaluated her initial impressions of the other woman. Carrie had seemed nice enough before, but Tulia decided she didn't like her very much after all. Not only did she sound almost arrogant in the way she spoke about herself, but she had brought two grieving people here to talk about their loved one's death without any warning. It was cruel.

"I don't know what I expected when you begged Jay and I to come out to lunch today, but it wasn't this," Veronica said, standing up suddenly. Her chair scraped across the patio's flagstones. "We don't need to listen to this. Jay?"

She looked down at her companion, who was still sitting. His lips turned down in a slight frown as he gazed at Carrie.

"I want to hear what she has to say," he said.

"She doesn't have anything worthwhile to say," Veronica snapped at him. "Let's go. We drove here together, and I'm not waiting around for you."

"Rebecca was a good swimmer," Jay said evenly. "She was on the diving team when we met in college. I spent all night thinking about what could have happened to her. If this woman thinks she knows something, I want to hear it."

Veronica hesitated. This close to her, Tulia could see the lines on her face and the bags under her eyes. She looked exhausted.

"Fine." She sat back down slowly and directed her words toward Carrie. "I'll listen to what you have to say, but it doesn't mean I'm happy about it. I knew you were up to *something* when you chased us down and asked us to come to lunch, but I didn't think it was something like this."

"I'm sorry, but I did say I had something important I wanted to share with you. Any other objections?" Carrie asked, looking around at them with a raised eyebrow. "No? Good. Well, as I'm sure some of you know, I returned to the beach before the snorkeling session ended. I went into the hut to take my sunscreen out of my beach bag and put it on. When I came out, I noticed two people swimming near the rocks where poor Rebecca lost her life. *Two* people. I didn't pay much attention to it at the time, and I don't know who else was with her, but I *know* what I saw. Rebecca wasn't alone when she died."

CHAPTER SEVEN

Samuel exchanged a glance with Marc, having another one of those split-second, silent conversations Tulia was envious of. He returned his attention to Carrie, and his brows pulled together as he said, "You didn't see any identifying traits? Not even the color of their bathing suit or whether the person who was with her was male or female?"

"I know I saw two people," Carrie said firmly. "But no, I couldn't see any details. They were still in the water, so I could only see their heads. With goggles and wet hair, everyone looks almost the same, especially from that distance."

"How certain are you that one of the people was Rebecca?" Samuel asked. "I'll be the first to admit that our instructor did a poor job of keeping tabs on everyone. But there were other people on the beach, albeit further down, and our own group was pretty dispersed. None of us knows for sure when Rebecca disappeared. Isn't it possible that the two people you saw by the rocks were completely unrelated to what happened to her?"

"Well, I know I didn't see her anywhere else after that," Carrie said. "And it was only about fifteen minutes before Travis called everyone in. I didn't think much of it at the time. I went back into the water briefly and just enjoyed the waves until everyone started returning."

"Let me get this straight," Veronica said slowly. "You're trying to tell me that somebody murdered my sister? And not only that—you're insinuating the killer was somebody in the group that went snorkeling." She looked around the table. "The group that includes all of us. In fact, everyone from the snorkeling group is here today, except for our instructor. I hope I'm wrong, but it feels to me like you are either accusing Jay—my sister's *fiancé*, who was supposed to be marrying her in two months—or me of murder, because I certainly don't think any of these other people knew her well enough to have a motive."

She gestured at Tulia's group. Hannah and Josiah were looking on, their expressions torn between fascination and embarrassment. Tulia felt bad for them. If they were fans of Carrie's books, the other woman had probably only invited them along so she would have some people on her side. She had to know what she was doing wasn't something most people would approve of.

"Oh, no, not at all," Carrie said. Her eyes widened, but Tulia couldn't tell if the expression of surprise on her face was real or manufactured. "No, I'm not even saying I think it was murder. I think it very well may have been an accidental death, but one that someone witnessed and covered up." She paused, something Tulia thought she inserted more for drama than anything else. "I think she and Travis went over to those rocks for a moment of privacy, and something happened. I think Travis—our snorkeling instructor, who should have been responsible for the safety of everyone in our group—allowed one of the people under his care to enter into a dangerous situation, and then tried to cover up his involvement in her death."

Slowly, Jay set his glass down and straightened up to look at Carrie.

"Why would Rebecca and Travis want a moment of privacy?" he asked, his voice icy. "That's my fiancée you're talking about."

"We all saw how much he was flirting with her," Carrie said, meeting his gaze unflinchingly. "And she seemed to enjoy it. And I know I'm not the only one who noticed that Travis wasn't exactly paying attention to the rest of us. In fact, I think there were plenty of times when I looked around and couldn't see him at all. He wasn't exactly the most professional of people."

"This is ridiculous," Veronica said. She stood again. "I know my sister, and she wouldn't sneak away with some snorkeling instructor for a 'moment of privacy.' I'm not going to listen to this. I'm out of here. Jay?"

"You're right. This was a waste of time." The two of them rose to their feet and walked away from the table. Carrie looked after them with a frown.

"They didn't take that well," she murmured.

"Did you expect them to?" Tulia asked, her voice sharper than she intended.

"I'm telling the truth about what I saw," Carrie said. "She wasn't alone by those rocks."

"Look," Samuel said. "I'm not saying we believe you or disbelieve you. But this isn't how you address something like this. If you truly saw her with someone else, you should have told the police, not blindsided Rebecca's family like this."

"I did tell the police," Carrie said. "But I wanted to make sure everyone else knew too. Haven't you ever had the urge to solve a mystery on your own? I finally have a real-life murder mystery right in front of me."

"Um, I thought you said it wasn't murder," Hannah cut in, looking a little nervous. "You said you thought her death was probably accidental."

"Right," Carrie said, waving her hand carelessly. "Same difference. I know what I saw. And I think I can get to the bottom of what happened, even without their help."

Tulia didn't need to do more than glance at her companions to know they felt the same as her. Whether or not Carrie was right about someone else being with Rebecca by the rocks, she was going about this all wrong.

After lunch, they left town to meet up with a guided tour of one of the island's volcanic beaches, which included a walk through the seaside forest. It was late by the time they returned to the resort, and Tulia felt a strange combination of exhaustion and anxious energy that she knew would lead to a racing mind if she tried to sleep right now.

She and Samuel walked with Marc and Violet up to their suites, where Violet said, "Well, I think we're going to turn in for the night. Tomorrow will be a busy day."

They said their goodnights, and Tulia and Samuel watched as their companions vanished into their suite. Tulia turned toward their door, then hesitated.

"Do you want to walk around with me for a little while?" she asked Samuel. "I know we spent the day on our feet, but I'm not going to be able to sleep. I can't get this whole mess with Carrie and Rebecca out of my mind."

"Sure," Samuel said. "Do you want to talk about it?"

"Yeah, that might help," she said. "I respect that Violet doesn't want the focus of this trip to be on a tragedy, and I even sort of agree with her, but that doesn't mean I can just stop thinking about it, even though I've been trying not to bring it up around her."

"I understand," Samuel said as he fell into step alongside her and they started walking back down the hall. They were heading toward the elevator, but at the last minute, Tulia decided to take the stairs. The second she stepped into the stairwell, she understood why Carrie kept using them instead of the elevator. The back wall of the stairwell was all glass, and the stairwell itself was decorated with fake ivy and real potted plants. It was easily the most beautiful stair-well she had ever been in.

"Okay, I know I said I wanted to have a mostly normal life after winning the lottery," Tulia muttered as they started down the stairs. "But I can see why people spend ridiculous amounts of money on things like this. Can you imagine living somewhere like this?"

"I think I would end up taking it for granted after a while," Samuel mused. "And it's probably a lot of work to keep these plants watered. I would end up killing them, and then my stairwell would just be filled with dead plants because I would forget to replace them."

She gave a reluctant laugh as she turned down the next flight of stairs. "Just crush all my dreams, why don't you. I'm glad you're a realist, though."

"I know you're worried about the money changing you," he said quietly. "But I don't think you need to be. Even if you did hire someone to build you a fancy stairwell like this, you'd still be the same old Tulia Blake, with terrible luck and a great sense of adventure. You would also just happen to have a stairwell filled with soon-to-be-dead plants."

"Ha-ha," she said, rolling her eyes. "Most people

would say someone who won the lottery has great lu—"

She broke off when the sound of a door opening beneath them caught her attention. She snapped her mouth shut out of long habit—she tried to keep her lottery winnings a secret, at least from anyone who wasn't a very close friend or immediate relative. People got strange when they learned about her winnings, and she didn't want it to become public knowledge.

"… might be sooner, might be longer. I don't know."

Tulia paused on the steps at the sound of the man's voice, and Samuel stopped beside her, a look of curiosity on his face. When she met his eyes, he mouthed, "Jay."

She blinked. She hadn't recognized the man's voice, both because he was speaking in low tones and because she hadn't heard much from him before.

"I probably won't be able to see you for weeks even after I get back. We're going to have the funeral, and I'll need to settle things with the house and the cars we owned together. It might be longer than that. Her mother still isn't doing well. I think they're waiting for her to either recover or pass on before telling her about her daughter." He paused while whoever he was talking to spoke to him. "I know. I feel bad, but there's nothing I can do. I'll keep you updated, and I'll try to get back sooner if I can. I love you."

The look she exchanged with Samuel was full of confusion on both ends as the man said goodbye and presumably ended the call. She heard another door open and then close, and the two of them continued on down the stairs. The stairwell had two doors at the bottom, one of which led outside, while the other led to the lobby. She wasn't sure which way Jay had gone.

"Somehow, I don't think he was talking to a sibling," Samuel muttered once they were sure they were alone.

"Me either," Tulia said softly. "That 'I love you' definitely didn't sound platonic. So what on earth is going on?"

CHAPTER EIGHT

She and Samuel stayed up late that night talking about their theories of what was going on with Rebecca's family. Although they didn't have anything solid, they both agreed that it seemed likely Jay had an affair partner, but the question of whether it had anything to do with Rebecca's death remained.

As a consequence of staying up late, they didn't get up until nearly ten the next morning. Tulia woke to a message on her phone from Violet letting her know that she and Marc were getting breakfast together on the patio near the pool. The message had been sent only twenty minutes ago, so she hurried to wake Samuel up and put on her bathing suit and some shorts with a t-shirt over it before going to meet their friends.

The cleaning cart was in the hall in front of Carrie's room when they stepped out of their suite, so Tulia ducked back inside to make sure they hadn't left too much of a mess behind. When she was done, they took the stairs down, and someone nearly opened the exterior door in Tulia's face. She jumped back just in time, only to come face-to-face with Travis. He was out of his work clothes, and he had two days' worth of stubble on his face.

"Sorry about that," he said, stepping back to let her by. Then he paused. "You're one of the people who went snorkeling the other day."

"Don't worry about it," she said. "And yeah, Samuel and I were both there."

Carrie's accusation came back to her, and she looked at Travis in a new light. Had he somehow been involved in Rebecca's death? He didn't look like a man with a huge secret. He just looked tired.

"I hope you're doing well," she said. She was a little curious about what the resort's response to Rebecca's death was, so she added, "They aren't blaming you for what happened, are they?"

He sighed. "They're doing an internal investigation. I'm suspended—with pay—for the time being. Even though they haven't officially blamed me for anything, I can tell all my coworkers think it's my fault she died. But we all live on the resort during the busy season, so I don't have anywhere else to go. I'm just trying to keep my head down. I feel horrible. Even if they don't fire me, I'm probably going to quit as soon as I find somewhere else to work. Someone *died* on my watch. I'll be lucky if I don't face a criminal charge for what happened."

"It sounds like now might be a good time to speak to an attorney," Samuel suggested. "Whatever happens, I wish you luck."

"Thanks," Travis said. He moved aside to let them through. Tulia glanced back to see him beginning to climb the stairs as they left the building.

Violet and Marc had claimed a small table with a sun umbrella next to the pool, along with a few lounge chairs and a stack of towels. Tulia and Samuel joined them, and Violet pushed a fruit platter over to them. Tulia snacked on the fresh fruits while she looked over the breakfast menu, and ordered a tall, iced coffee to go with her meal. She still felt tired and didn't know whether jet lag or her late night was more to blame.

They discussed their plans for the day as they ate, and after enjoying their food, they slipped into the pool. The water was the perfect temperature, though Tulia wished the beach hadn't been shut down. There was something magical about the ocean that the pool, with its sharp chlorine smell and crowded waters couldn't match.

She and Violet were leaning against the edge of the pool, discussing the pros and cons of finding a beach that wasn't closed and paying for some surfing lessons when a sharp scream made them both look up just in time to see a woman tumble from one of the balconies that looked out over the courtyard.

Violet let out a shriek as the woman crashed into one of the large bushes that lined the building. Samuel and Marc were on their feet in an instant and ran over to her as Tulia and Violet pulled themselves out of the pool. Dripping chlorinated water, Tulia raced over to where the woman had fallen. Samuel was helping her out of the bush, and Tulia froze when she saw who it was.

"Carrie?" She forced her surprise to the side enough to ask, "Are you okay? Do you need us to call an ambulance?"

"I… I think I'm all right," Carrie said, looking down at herself as if to make sure her arms and her legs were still there. A crowd was gathering around them, and the air was filled with worried murmurs and whispers. "Nothing's broken."

"How did you fall?" Violet asked, her eyes wide

with concern. "Did the balcony give way?" She looked up at the balcony. Tulia followed her gaze, but she could see that the railing was still intact.

"No." Carrie took a deep breath. "No … someone pushed me."

Tulia's own eyes widened, and she looked up again, half expecting to see someone leering over the edge of the woman's balcony.

"Did you see who it was?" Samuel asked. Marc looked up at the balcony too, then broke away from their group and headed towards the stairs without a word.

Carrie shook her head. "I didn't. I was looking out over the balcony when I heard someone come in. The cleaner had just left, and I thought they were coming back for something, so I didn't bother to look over my shoulder. The next thing I know, someone shoved me *hard,* and I lost my balance and went over the rail."

"If they're still in there, Marc will find them," Samuel said.

"Are you sure you're all right?" Tulia asked. "That was quite the fall. You're lucky you landed in a bush."

"I know, I am, aren't I?" Carrie said with a shudder. "My heart's still pounding. I might have a few scratches, but other than that, I'm fine. I hope your friend is okay—if whoever pushed me is still up there, he might get hurt."

Violet looked up at the balcony, worry making her face look drawn and pale. "He knows what he's doing," she said, though she didn't sound at all certain.

Carrie frowned. "Does he work for law enforcement?"

Violet shook her head, her eyes still on the balcony. "Private investigator."

Tulia frowned, glancing at Samuel. She had forgotten to ask him why he and Marc hadn't mentioned their career path at lunch the day before. The cat was out of the bag now.

A few moments later, Marc looked out over the balcony. "Sorry, but there's no one in the room," he called down. "I haven't touched anything—the door was already open when I got up here."

"Do you think I should call the police?" Carrie asked. "I'm not sure what they could do if whoever pushed me is already long gone."

Tulia glanced around them at the crowd of concerned guests. From the other side of the court-yard, a handful of employees were hurrying over.

"I don't think you'll have a choice," she said. "I doubt the staff is going to let something like this slide without doing everything by the book, especially not after what happened to Rebecca."

Carrie seemed to soak in the attention from the resort's employees and the other guests once the initial shock wore off. She waited on a lounge chair in the shade while one of the staff called the police, and told her tale to anyone who would listen.

They all waited with her, and everyone in the courtyard talked to the police when they arrived, even if only briefly. Tulia, Violet, and one other woman were the only ones who had actually seen Carrie fall, and the officer wrote down their accounts of what had happened.

Tulia wasn't sure what it meant that this was the second potentially fatal occurrence at the resort since they had arrived. Rebecca's death could have been an accident, but this?

What happened to Carrie was attempted murder.

CHAPTER NINE

When the chaos of Carrie's fall died down and the police left, Tulia and her friends invited her to join them at their table by the pool. She was still shaken, and Tulia felt bad knowing that she was here on her own. Traveling alone was all well and good, but she knew firsthand how much the presence of a few friendly faces could help when something unexpected happened.

"Are you sure you're all right?" Tulia asked.

"We would be happy to take you to an urgent care center if you don't want to go to a hospital," Samuel added.

"I'm fine," Carrie said. "Really. I landed right in that bush. I was lucky. I have a couple of scratches, but that's it."

"What are you going to do now?" Marc asked. "We can take turns making sure you aren't alone until you manage to book a stay at another resort."

Carrie frowned. "Why would I go to another resort?"

Tulia exchanged a look with the others. "Because someone here tried to kill you?" she said. "You're not seriously planning on staying, are you?"

"Of course I am. This is the most interesting thing that has ever happened to me. I'll be careful, but there's no way I'm leaving without getting to the bottom of this."

"Your life could be in danger," Samuel said. "Leaving would be the smart thing to do. Let the police handle this."

"Look, I'm staying," Carrie said, crossing her arms. "I appreciate that you are worried about my safety, but this doesn't concern you."

"I understand how hard it is to walk away from —" Tulia broke off when her cell phone started ringing. She glanced down at the screen and winced. She was supposed to call her parents today. The time difference made it hard to find a good time, but they had settled on early evening, Michigan time.

Which meant midday Hawaiian time. She had

completely forgotten, between Carrie's fall and the subsequent chat with the police.

"I'm sorry," she said. "Do you mind if I take this? I won't be long, but my parents were going to do a video call with Cicero, and I'm sure he misses me."

"Of course," Samuel said. "Take as much time as you need."

"Say hi to that cute little bird of yours for us," Violet said with a smile. Carrie just looked confused as Tulia grabbed her phone and got up, sliding her finger across the screen to answer it.

She greeted her parents and then pressed the button to change the voice call into a video call. She angled the phone so she was standing with the view of the ocean behind her. Her mother's reaction did not disappoint, and she *oohed* and *ahhed* over the scenery for a few moments.

"You know, I would be happy to treat all three of us to a vacation like this," Tulia offered. Her lips tugged up in a smile as she saw the familiar stubborn expression cross both her parents' faces.

"It's not your job to spend money on us, sweetie," her father said. "Though we appreciate the offer."

"Besides, if we all went on a trip, who would take care of Cicero? He misses you, but he's been doing well.

I've been spending extra time with him." She turned the phone around so Tulia could see Cicero standing on his play stand. As her mother moved closer with the phone, the bird turned one of his bright eyes toward her. She heard him whistle, and she whistled back at him, not caring if it got her weird looks from the other guests.

"Hey there, Cicero. How are you doing? Are they taking good care of you? I hope you don't miss me too much. I'll be back in a week. I promise, you and I are going to go on a big adventure together soon."

She wasn't worried about how the bird would adjust to living in Loon Bay. He had come along with her on her previous visits, and he had his own dedicated perch at Samuel and Marc's office. As long as she continued to spend plenty of time with him, he would be happy wherever they were.

"He's doing fine," her mother assured her. "I think he's a little bored, since he won't let your father or I put the harness on him so we can take him outside, but we've been leaving the TV on for him and giving him plenty of healthy snacks. How's your trip going?"

"It's been … interesting," Tulia said. She hesitated, knowing that her parents would want to know about what happened to Rebecca, but also knowing it would just drive them crazy with worry if they learned about it while she was still here. She decided to hold off on saying anything until she knew more. "It's absolutely beautiful here. The water is amazing, and all the food we've had so far has been great. I can see why Hawaii is such a popular vacation destination. I think I'd like to come back some day."

"That's great," her mother said. "Take lots of pictures for us, okay?"

"And bring us back some souvenirs. We need more magnets to put on our fridge. Remember, it's your job to get us one from every state."

"I won't forget," she said with a smile.

"We'll let you go now," her mother said. "I'm sure you have a busy schedule. We miss you, sweetie. We'll be there at the airport to pick you up when you fly back. Just let us know if your flight times change."

Tulia said her goodbyes and ended the call. She returned to the table, a bittersweet feeling lingering in her chest. She was going to miss her parents when she moved out of state, and she knew the feeling would be mutual. She was planning on visiting them regularly, and would insist on flying them out to see her too, even if they tried to object to her buying their plane tickets. It would be hard to adjust to only seeing them sporadically, but at the same time, she knew neither of them would want her to delay living her dreams just so she could stay close to them.

There was a whole world out there, and while Loon Bay might not be the most exotic location she could move to, figuring out her life with Samuel was a whole new type of adventure, and she was looking forward to it.

When she reclaimed her seat, Carrie looked irritated, and no one else was talking.

"What did I miss?"

"We've just been expressing our worries," Violet said. "I swear, she's just as stubborn as Marc and Samuel are." She shot Tulia an unimpressed look. "And you too, come to think of it. None of you seem to understand the concept of avoiding dangerous things."

"I'm a mystery writer," Carrie said. "And I'm elbow deep in a real mystery right now. This could be career changing for me."

"Like I said, you're just as bad as them," Violet grumbled, jabbing her thumb toward the guys. "At least they have an excuse. They're private investigators—they're helping people. You're just writing stories. Is it really worth risking your life for?"

Carrie looked at Samuel and Marc with a new light in her eyes. "The two of you are private investigators? I was a little distracted when Violet mentioned it before."

"We are," Samuel said. "We didn't bring it up before because we knew it would likely lead to someone asking us to get involved in figuring out what happened to Rebecca, and we have been trying to keep this trip work free."

"I know now isn't the time, but I would love to interview both of you before you leave," Carrie said. "I should get going for now, though. I signed up for a tour of the island that leaves in about half an hour." She turned to Tulia. "I'll find you later. We have *got* to have a real talk. You know some interesting people."

"Let me give you my number," Tulia said.

Carrie passed her phone over for Tulia to type her number in. She slipped the phone back into her purse and rose from her chair, saying a final goodbye to the table as a whole. After shooting a wary look at her balcony, she turned around and walked away, heading for the lobby doors. Tulia watched her go, more worried than she had let on. She respected Carrie's choice to stay, but that didn't mean it wasn't dangerous. Someone had tried to kill her, and she didn't think the other woman was taking it seriously enough.

"You know, maybe it would be better if *we* found somewhere else to stay," Violet said quietly once they were alone again. "One person already died here, and another one almost did. I'm not sure how safe this resort is."

"I'm open to doing whatever the rest of you want, but I'm not sure if I trust anything Carrie says," Marc said.

"What did you find when you went up to her room?" Samuel asked.

"Nothing," Marc said. "Which doesn't prove anything, but the entire incident as a whole feels off, especially when you factor in what happened at lunch yesterday."

"What do you mean?" Tulia asked. "Do you think she's lying about someone pushing her off the balcony?"

"I'm saying we should consider the possibility that she jumped."

"Why would she do that?" Violet gasped. "She could have *died.*"

"But she didn't," Marc pointed out. "She landed safely in a bush. She wasn't injured at all. If someone pushed her unexpectedly, she wouldn't have had time to prepare for a proper landing or decide where she wanted to fall. It's possible she got lucky, but when you combine that with her other actions and her relaxed response after what happened, it makes me wonder just how truthful she's being."

Samuel frowned. "She does seem a little too relaxed about almost being pushed to her death."

"Okay, but *why* would she jump?" Tulia asked. "It doesn't make any sense."

"I'm with her," Violet said. "She would have to be crazy. Why on earth would someone leap off of their balcony for no reason?"

"For the attention," Marc said. "That whole farce with lunch—she went to great lengths to get Veronica and Jay there and gave a dramatic reveal about seeing someone else in the water with Rebecca instead of speaking to one of them privately. And now with this… It feels almost like she's trying to insert herself into that poor woman's death."

"What she did at lunch bothered me too," Samuel said. "I looked her up last night and read the synopsis of some of the books she's written. They all seem to be based on real-life crimes. She went so far as to interview some of the victims' families and some of the perpetrators. It's possible she's planning on writing about this and thinks her own involvement will make for a more interesting story."

Tulia opened her mouth to defend the other woman, then closed it again. Blindsiding Veronica and Jay at lunch yesterday had been going too far, and everything Marc had pointed out about the odd circumstances surrounding her fall from the balcony rang true too.

"It sounds extreme," she said slowly. "But she *did* say she came here to get inspiration for her next book. Do you think she was lying about seeing someone else with Rebecca by the rocks, or was that part true?"

"I'm not sure," Marc said. "And I know we promised not to get involved with this, but I think we should keep an eye on Carrie. She could do more harm than good if this is all a publicity play for her books."

"I agree," Samuel said as Tulia nodded.

Violet sighed, then said, "All right. I can't insist that the two of you ignore this completely, but I don't want it taking over the rest of the trip. You need a *break¸* Marc. So don't let this consume you. Deal?"

"Deal," Marc said, laying an arm around his wife's shoulders and pulling her close. "We'll investigate on the side, but you'll still get the vacation of a lifetime, I promise."

CHAPTER TEN

They left for the city after breakfast. This was their day for self-guided exploring, and Tulia was a little surprised by how easy it was to put everything else on the back burner and just live in the moment. Kahului was gorgeous. They visited every shop that caught their eye, buying souvenirs for their friends and family at home. They stopped by a museum, and then got street food for a late lunch. They ate their food in a park that was so beautiful Tulia was sure every park she visited later would fall flat by comparison.

On their way back to the resort that evening they picked up a pizza, and then sat in Marc and Violet's suite, chatting, looking over the souvenirs, and stuffing themselves full of food.

This was what a vacation was supposed to be. No worries, just having fun.

The next day dawned overcast and muggy. They got breakfast in the resort's dining area instead of by the pool and went over their plans for the day. Violet had expressed an interest in another nature walk, so they decided to spend the day at a state park that was about an hour's drive away. They would need to stop at a store to buy a cooler and snacks on their way, but first, they needed their morning burst of energy, and the tea she'd had before just wasn't cutting it for Tulia.

She finished the cold floral tea and went up to the coffee bar to get a cup of coffee to top it off with. The jet lag hadn't been too bad, since she had established a good sleep schedule right away, but she still felt off. She had never been somewhere with such a major time difference before, and it was odd to think that while she was just waking up, her parents were already more than halfway through their day.

While she waited in line for the coffee, her eyes roamed over the room and landed on two people huddled together by the far wall, between a tall plant and a long table with some sort of informational display on it. She frowned as she recognized Veronica and Jay, and wondered why they were still here. She felt guilty enough for continuing to enjoy her vacation after someone drowned, but Rebecca had been Veronica's sister, and Jay's fiancée. Why were they still at the resort, or in Hawaii at all?

Tulia's curiosity got the better of her. She grabbed her coffee, put in a dash of creamer, and stirred it as she wandered casually toward them. The table they were next to was a display about the local island's history, which gave her an excuse to linger as she strained her ears to hear what they were saying.

"I've made up my mind. I'm leaving tomorrow," Jay said. "I'm not going to keep up this farce any longer."

"And *I'm* telling *you* to wait out the week. My mother isn't doing well. The doctors think she only has a couple of days left. If you go back home, someone is going to notice Rebecca isn't with you. They're going to ask why, and eventually it will get back to Mom when some tender-hearted cousin decides they can't keep their mouth shut."

"Your issues with your family aren't my problem anymore," Jay said. "I was only here for Rebecca. I don't even *like* you. Why should I keep my fiancée's death a secret?"

"Because my mother is *dying* and she doesn't need to know one of her daughters passed away," Veronica hissed. "Just keep your mouth shut and enjoy the rest of your trip."

"Enjoy my trip when my fiancée *died* three days ago," Jay replied slowly. "That's rich. You really don't care at all."

"She's my sister. Of course I care," Veronica said shortly. "But it doesn't change the fact that if you go home alone, it will only raise questions that we can't have people asking. Not yet. Or do you want to be responsible for a dying woman learning that her favorite child preceded her into an early grave?"

"I don't think keeping Rebecca's death a secret is the right thing to do," Jay said. "But I'll keep my head down and won't talk to anyone we both know. I'm sick of being here. I want to go home."

"You want to go home to your *girlfriend*, that's what you mean," Veronica said darkly.

Tulia glanced over in time to see Jay freeze, his back going ramrod straight. "I have no idea what you're talking about."

Veronica's lips curled up into a cruel smile. "Our mother pays for my and Rebecca's phone bills, but when she was put into hospice care and I got power of attorney, I took all of that over. Rebecca added you to her phone plan a year ago. I have access to every outgoing call and message you've made. I know you've been seeing someone else, if not for the entirety of your relationship with my sister, then for most of it. I know everything, Jay. I know you talked Rebecca out of a prenup, and that you were planning on swindling her out of a good portion of her inheritance. I know the two of you own the house she bought, and your name is on both of the vehicles she owned. I know you have a shared bank account with her with quite a lot of money in it. If you go home and let slip what happened before my mother passes away, I won't hesitate to take all the proof I have and share it with our attorney to make sure you get nothing from Rebecca's passing."

Jay remained frozen for a moment. "If … if you really know what you think you know, then why didn't you say anything to her?"

"My sister and I don't have that kind of relationship," Veronica said. "I was content with letting her make her own mistakes. But I'm not going to let you mess this up for me. After Mom passes on, you can do what you want. We'll both go our separate ways and never have to talk to each other again. But until then, shut up, stay here, and play the grieving fiancé whenever you're in public. Got it?"

Jay gave a stiff nod. Tulia picked up a picture of Haleakala Crater, the dormant volcano in Maui's

Haleakala National Park, as he walked past her. She heard Veronica let out a quiet, annoyed sound, and then the other woman walked away as well.

Tulia waited another moment, then returned to her table, shaken.

"Please tell me you weren't spying on those two," Violet murmured to her as she sat down.

"I was."

Violet sighed. "Samuel and Marc called it. I've said it before, but you are just as bad as they are."

Beside her, Samuel smiled. "Tulia loves mysteries as much as I do, and that's not a bad thing. What did you learn?"

"Remember that conversation we overheard Jay having on his phone? Well, our suspicions were right. He has a secret girlfriend, and Veronica knew about it. She's using it to threaten him into staying at the resort. From the sound of it, Veronica and Rebecca's family is quite well off, and she told Jay he wouldn't get anything from Rebecca if he went back home early."

Marc blinked. "Why? Why would she want him to stay here?"

Tulia grimaced. "I'm not sure exactly, but it sounds like Veronica's mother is in hospice care and is expected to pass away soon. She doesn't want Jay to go home and let slip what happened to Rebecca. She said it would cause her mother more pain, but then she also said something about Jay not messing this up for her. I don't know what she was talking about when she said that."

"This takes family drama to a new level," Samuel muttered. "Though it does explain why they're both still here. I can almost understand her motivations, if she truly wants to save her mother extra pain on her deathbed, but it still seems cruel. Not only are they keeping an important secret from her, but now she won't have either of her daughters with her in her final moments."

Tulia nodded, sipping her coffee and making a face when she found it was only lukewarm. She wasn't sure how she felt about the thought of Veronica keeping her sister's death from their mother. If the woman really was only hours or days from passing away, she could see how Veronica might consider it a kindness not to worsen her emotional pain in her last moments. It still felt wrong to her, though, and nothing about Veronica's attitude had seemed kind.

CHAPTER ELEVEN

They put their conversation on hold while they returned to their suites to start packing for their day trip. They had picked up a few cheap, string backpacks while they were out the day before, and Tulia packed her bathing suit, a couple of water bottles, and a charging pack for her phone into hers, along with her wallet so she didn't have to carry her purse around. Samuel was changing for the hike, so she knocked on the bathroom door and said, "I'm going to go pull the car around and ask the person at the front desk if they know where we can go to buy a cooler and some ice."

"All right," he called back. "I'll meet you down there in a few minutes."

She put her backpack on and left the room. Once

she reached the bottom of the stairs, she made her way over to the front desk to ask about the closest stores that would have what they needed. The man who was working there pulled out a local map and showed her where she could find a supermarket that should have everything they were looking for.

"Make sure you bring plenty of water," he added. "A lot of tourists underestimate the heat and how much it dehydrates them on long hikes, even with the humidity. And I suggest bringing some umbrellas as well. It's supposed to rain in the next hour or two. It shouldn't rain for long, but when the clouds burst, you'll be miserable without some way to stay dry."

She thanked him for his advice and grabbed the map, then went out the front door and located the rental car. It was boiling hot inside, so she set her bag down on the passenger seat and turned the air-conditioning up, then put the windows down so the interior could cool off faster. Then she reversed out of the parking spot and pulled up under the overhang in front of the resort's front doors. She let the car idle as she picked up her phone, intending to check on her blog while she waited for the others. She wanted to write a blog post about her time in Hawaii, but she couldn't decide if she wanted to do a two-part post or wait until the trip was over and do one big one.

A shadow fell across the open driver's side window, and she looked up to see Jay staring down at her.

"Excuse me," he said. "Your name is Tulia, right? Carrie introduced us a few days ago at the bistro, and we went snorkeling together before that."

"Yes," she said slowly. She started to put her phone down, then thought better of it and kept it in her hand. "How can I help you?"

"Is it true that the men you are traveling with are private investigators?"

"It is. Do you mind if I ask how you know that?"

"Carrie told me," he said. He rushed on before she could ask more. "Do you think they would be willing to hear me out? I think I know something about what happened to Rebecca, but I need a second opinion before I go to the police."

Tulia hesitated. They had promised Violet they wouldn't work during this trip, but she knew Samuel and Marc wouldn't turn down someone who was asking for their help.

"We can ask them," she said. "They're supposed to meet me down here soon."

"Carrie said you're on the same floor she is. She's helping me with this, and I'd like to meet with everyone in her room. Do you mind coming upstairs with me now? It's time sensitive."

She hesitated, then rolled the windows up and shut the car off before getting out. She grabbed her bag from the passenger's seat and shut the door. The car would be fine here for a few minutes. Jay sounded serious, and while she wasn't quite sure what was going on, it seemed important.

"Let's go," she said.

They walked indoors, past the front desk, and toward the elevator. The elevator doors closed behind them, and she was suddenly very aware that she was alone in an enclosed space with someone who was connected to a possible homicide.

She breathed a sigh of relief when the elevator came to a stop and the doors opened with a ding. He gestured for her to go out first.

She walked down the hall with him slightly behind her, second-guessing herself. Was this some sort of trap? Was *he* the person who had killed Rebecca and attempted to kill Carrie?

Her eyes were focused on the door to her suite at the end of the hall, and she hoped that she hadn't somehow missed Samuel, Marc, and Violet. She hadn't seen them in the lobby, but it was possible they had gone down the stairs and were wondering where *she* had gotten to.

"You go get your friends. I'll tell Carrie we're going to meet now," he said as they approached the author's door.

Tulia nodded, then glanced at Carrie's door again and frowned. It was partially open.

"What is it?" Jay asked.

"Why would she leave her door open like that?" Tulia asked quietly, her voice barely above a whisper.

"She agreed to help me," he said. "She probably left it open because she knew I would be back soon."

"Someone tried to kill her yesterday. She wouldn't leave the door to her suite open like this."

Unless Marc was right and Carrie had been lying about the murder attempt.

Jay stared at her, surprise and disbelief written across his face. "What are you talking about? Someone tried to *kill* her?"

"She didn't tell you?"

"I've hardly spoken to her, other than to ask if she was serious about seeing someone else with Rebecca while we were snorkeling. I barely know the woman, but she seemed like the only other one who was inter-ested in getting to the truth of things. I ran into her in the hall after breakfast today and asked if she would help me with something. That was when she mentioned that the two men you were with are private eyes and suggested we involve the four of you too. I was heading through the lobby to go upstairs when I saw you go outside. She was coming up here to wait for me."

Tulia hesitated, then moved toward the partially open door. She didn't know what to believe, but if someone really *had* attacked Carrie, then the open door could be a sign that the woman was in danger.

"Go down to the last door on the right and knock on it. Tell Samuel that I'm in Carrie's room," Tulia said. She looked at Jay, who hesitated. "Please. If you want us to help you, go get him. I need to make sure she's okay."

He nodded and hurried down the hall. Tulia turned toward the door and raised her fist to knock, but paused. If someone really *was* after Carrie, the last thing she wanted to do was give her presence away. Instead of knocking, she stepped up to the door and pushed it gently open. It swung inward without a noise, and Tulia looked inside the suite.

Carrie's suite was much like hers, if a little messier. She didn't see anyone in the living area, so she stepped inside and glanced toward the bedroom.

The door was closed, as was the door to the bathroom.

Movement brought her eyes around to the balcony. The door was open, and through the sheer curtains, she saw two forms sitting outside on it.

She moved across the room quietly and pushed the curtain aside. Carrie and Veronica looked up at the motion, startled. They were seated across from each other at the little wicker table, a pitcher of water between them.

"There you are," Carrie said. "Did Jay find you already? Are the others coming too?"

"He's going to get them," Tulia said. "What's going on here?"

She looked from Veronica back to Carrie. The author was the one who responded. "I think I figured out who the killer is," she said. "I wanted to get everyone together so I could lay out my theories."

Tulia frowned. That wasn't what Jay had said. He had made it sound like *he* was the one who wanted to talk to them.

"This isn't a television drama," Veronica snapped. "Just spit it out. I'm sick of waiting around so you can show off to your so-called fans. This is my sister we're talking about. If you think someone killed her, then I want to know who it is."

"We have to do this properly," Carrie said. "Like I told Jay, two of Tulia's friends are private investigators. They'll be able to tell me if I'm on the right track or not."

"I don't care," Veronica ground out. "I'm tired of this. Tell me, or I'm leaving. Right now. I don't think you're anything more than some crazy woman with delusions of importance, and if you want to prove me wrong, this is your only chance."

When Carrie made no move to say anything, Veronica stood up. Carrie rose too, saying, "No, no. Don't go. I'll tell you." She took a deep breath. "The snorkeling instructor, Travis Feeney, is the reason your sister died, and I have proof."

CHAPTER TWELVE

Veronica blinked and sat back down.

"You really have proof?"

Tulia had to admit that she was intrigued too. There were only two chairs on the balcony, so she had to remain standing, but she moved a little closer to the table as she listened.

"I took the liberty of talking to some of the other employees," Carrie said. "Travis is currently on leave while they are doing an internal investigation. One of the other employees told me this wasn't the first issue they've had with him. He's made some mistakes with the equipment before, one of which led to someone getting injured during a surfing class, and he's had some bad reviews from previous groups saying he didn't give them proper instruction and wasn't available when they needed help."

"None of this is proof that he murdered her," Veronica said, narrowing her eyes.

"I never said it was murder," Carrie pointed out. "I think it was simple negligence, just like I said at the bistro a couple of days ago. It was his job to keep everyone safe. I think he was on the rocks with her when she fell and hit her head, and when he couldn't get her out of the water himself, he returned to the beach and pretended he didn't know what was going on. He was indirectly responsible for her death but is trying to cover it up so he doesn't get into any legal trouble."

"That sounds plausible, but I'm still not seeing any proof," Tulia said. "And what about what happened to you? Someone pushed you off your balcony, Carrie."

"That was him too," Carrie said. "He's an employee here. He would have had access to my room with a master key. He must have heard I was asking about him, and he decided to take matters into his own hands to keep me quiet."

"So he covered up an accidental death with an attempted murder?" Tulia asked skeptically.

"This is absurd and a waste of time," Veronica

said, rising to her feet. "I'm leaving. I thought you might have some real information, but this is useless."

"No, wait!" Carrie jumped to her feet to follow Veronica as she stomped back through the suite, toward the door.

Tulia had left the door to the room open when she entered the room, not wanting to be trapped inside if someone really was in here to kill Carrie. The door was still open, and before Veronica reached it, Jay stepped over the threshold, followed closely by Samuel.

"What's going on?" he asked, looking between the three of them before his concerned gaze lingered on Tulia. "Jay said he wanted to talk to Marc and me. Marc and Violet already went downstairs and are probably looking for you right now, but I was still in the suite when he knocked."

"I'm not sure if there's anything left to say," Tulia admitted with an apologetic look at Jay. "It's just the same stuff we heard at the bistro."

"I agree," Veronica said. "This was a waste of time."

"Hold on," Jay said, moving to block Tulia's path as she tried to leave the room. Samuel's expression darkened.

"Let her go by."

"I'm trying to explain," Jay said. "I'm not here for whatever reason Carrie made up. She has her own theories, but she agreed to get everyone together to talk. I have something important to say, and I need some competent witnesses when I do it." He took a deep breath. "I know who killed Rebecca." His gaze focused on Veronica. "It was you. You murdered your sister."

Veronica took a step back.

"You're insane. You're trying to shift the blame off of yourself, aren't you? You are the one who was having an affair, the one who was using her. You never cared about her. She found out, didn't she? You killed her to keep her quiet and to make sure all those years you spent with her weren't a waste."

"I'll admit that what I did to Rebecca was horrible," Jay said. "I did use her. I was never in love with her. But that doesn't mean I ever wanted her to *die*. For all of her flaws and naivety, Rebecca was a good person. I might not have loved her, but I knew her very well, and I did care for her in my own way. That's why, after the discussion I had with you this morning, Veronica, I called your aunt."

Veronica's face paled. "You what? What did you tell her?"

"I told her Rebecca died, and I shared some of my

concerns with her. Your aunt was kind enough to tell me the details of your mother's will. She's splitting her estate between her two children. You and Rebecca were supposed to each receive half of her wealth when she died. I remembered what you said this morning, about me not 'wrecking this' for you, and your insistence your mother didn't learn what happened. You killed Rebecca so you could get the full inheritance, didn't you?"

Carrie gasped, but she looked more fascinated than horrified. Tulia inched away from Veronica and eased past Jay so she was standing next to Samuel, who was gazing at Veronica with a hard expression. The woman's jaw clenched.

"You have no idea what you're talking about."

"It makes sense, in a twisted sort of way," Jay said. "If your mother learned about what happened to Rebecca before she passed on, she might want to make changes to her will, maybe donate Rebecca's half to a charity or another relative. Or maybe she would suspect what you did. That's why you're so worried about her finding out, isn't it?"

"I can't believe I missed it," Carrie cut in before Veronica could respond. "Of course. It all makes sense now. Whoever pushed me off the balcony *must* have been connected to what happened to Rebecca.

It's too much of a coincidence otherwise. I told you at lunch I saw a second person with your sister by the rocks, Veronica. Then, not even twenty-four hours later, someone tried to kill me to keep me quiet. It was you all along!"

"I don't need to talk to any of you," Veronica said. She tried to shove Jay aside, but he braced himself and blocked the exit. Unlike when he did the same to Tulia, Samuel didn't interfere.

"Can you call Marc and ask him to get up here?" he asked quietly, glancing at Tulia.

She took out her phone and dialed Marc's number. Veronica tried to snatch the phone out of Tulia's hand, but Jay pushed her arm down.

"I just don't understand how you could do it," Jay said. "She was your *sister*. She loved you. She never would have hurt you. Rebecca was the best person in your entire family, and she got the short end of the stick from everyone."

Veronica let out a laugh with no mirth in it at all. "You think *she* got the short end of the stick? She was everyone's favorite. Sweet Rebecca, the baby of the family. I was the oldest, the one they were most strict with. The second I graduated from college, all financial help from our parents stopped. But Rebecca? She continued getting a stipend even years later. When

Dad died, Rebecca was the one who gave his eulogy, and he left her his journals and all of the possessions he knew she loved. Mom gave *me* power of attorney when she got sick because she didn't want dear, sweet Rebecca to have to handle making the hard choices when her mother was dying. And my aunt was wrong. I *saw* my mother's will. Rebecca was getting more than half of everything, while I got the short end of the stick *again* because I make more money than she does and don't 'need' the inheritance as much."

She fell silent, breathing heavily. Carrie was gazing at her in fascination. "You really did kill her, didn't you?"

"I didn't mean to," Veronica snapped. "Despite all of that, I was planning on keeping my mouth shut like I always did. When I saw her swim away and climb on those rocks, I joined her. I was actually going to tell her about *you*, Jay. Your affair. I should have done it a long time ago, but I was feeling petty and mean, and I wanted to tell her then, to wreck her trip. But before I could speak, she told me she was feeling guilty about Mom's will and that she promised to give me a part of her inheritance on top of what I was getting. She *pitied* me. I just… I lost control. I shoved her, and she slipped off the rock. She hit her head and then she didn't move, and I saw everyone else beginning to return to the beach, so I slipped into the water and pretended I had no idea what happened." Veronica took a deep breath. "I didn't mean to kill her. She was my sister. But it was a type of karma, I think. She was the golden child for so long. It was my turn to have everything."

Tulia ended the call with Marc before he could answer. She'd heard enough and started dialing the number for the police instead. She noticed belatedly as Samuel had his own phone out, held subtly in his hand. She could see the screen from where she was standing, and realized he was recording the conversation. No wonder he had asked her to make the call instead of doing it himself—he was getting the evidence they needed to make sure Veronica faced justice for what she had done.

"Did you try to kill Carrie too?" Samuel asked. His voice was measured and calm instead of accusatory.

"I didn't think anyone was suspicious about Rebecca's death until she sprung it on us at the bistro," Veronica said, glaring at the other woman. "I didn't realize she was completely incompetent until later. I thought she might be onto something, and when I walked by her room and saw her standing at the balcony through her open door, it seemed like the perfect chance to get rid of the only witness to my sister's death."

Carrie looked stunned. "I really was involved in a murder mystery. I can't wait to start writing about it."

Tulia wondered if this was what Violet felt like when Samuel and Marc tracked down a killer instead of running in the opposite direction. At least *they* had a good excuse. Carrie, she was pretty sure, was just insane.

EPILOGUE

Tulia walked along the beach, her legs and arms shaking. Violet hurried to meet her, her wide eyes full of worry and excitement.

"Are you okay? How was that? It looked like a lot of fun."

Tulia couldn't have stopped grinning if she tried. "It was terrifying and exhilarating. You should try it."

"No way," Violet said. "Parasailing is not for me. I'd be terrified the whole time I was up there. It's bad enough having to worry about the three crazy people I'm traveling with—I don't need to be worried about my *own* safety on top of it."

She looked up and shaded her eyes as she gazed out over the ocean, where Samuel and Marc were both still up in the air, dangling beneath parasail wings being dragged along behind boats. It was the second to last day of their trip, and after Veronica's arrest, things had calmed down enough that they could relax and enjoy the slice of paradise that Hawaii was. Carrie had flown out the day before, and Tulia felt a little bad that she kept brushing off the woman's request for an interview, but she didn't like Carrie very much. She was too quick to benefit from other people's tragedies and seemed more focused on herself than on the people around her. It was a good reminder that just because someone shared some of her interests didn't mean that they were compatible as friends.

She might not have made a new friend while she was here, but she felt a lot closer to the ones she had come with. They had gone through something big and had come out stronger on the other side.

"It will be nice to get home," she mused quietly as she tracked Samuel and Marc's progress across the sky. "But I'm going to miss this place. I'm glad the three of you could come along."

"Thank you for inviting us," Violet said. "I can see what you like about traveling so much, though hopefully next time I go somewhere, it will be a little bit less … exciting."

"I'm never quite sure if I have terrible or amazing

luck," Tulia admitted. "But unfortunately, this trip was pretty much par for the course for me. I can't say I've ever had a boring trip to someplace new."

"Do you miss it?" Violet asked. "Being on the road? Always going somewhere new?"

"I do," Tulia admitted. "I still plan on taking another road trip at some point, but I want to get settled in Loon Bay first, and I want to take some other trips in the meantime. I was thinking of going to Alaska sometime this summer. Do you think Marc would be upset if I stole Samuel away for another week?"

Violet grinned. "Please do. That man needs to work less. I'm so glad he found someone like you, Tulia. You're good for him."

"He's good for me too," Tulia said. He and Marc were coming back toward the beach now. She smiled and waved as they sailed through the sky. "There was a lot that I enjoyed about my trip, but finding him was the best of all."

Made in the USA
Coppell, TX
15 November 2023